Judy Moody
and the Bad Luck Charm

Judy Moody
and the Bad Luck Charm

Megan McDonald

illustrated by
Peter H. Reynolds

CANDLEWICK PRESS

official stuff

Text copyright © 2012 by Megan McDonald
Illustrations copyright © 2012 by Peter H. Reynolds
Judy Moody font copyright © 2003 by Peter H. Reynolds

Judy Moody®. Judy Moody is a registered trademark of Candlewick Press, Inc.

First paperback edition in this format 2018

Library of Congress Catalog Card Number 2011048352
ISBN 978-0-7636-3451-3 (hardcover)
ISBN 978-1-5362-0080-5 (paperback)

18 19 20 21 22 23 BVG 10 9 8 7 6 5 4 3 2

Printed in Berryville, VA, U.S.A.

This book was typeset in Stone Informal and Judy Moody.
The illustrations were done in watercolor, tea, and ink.

Candlewick Press
99 Dover Street
Somerville, Massachusetts 02144

visit us at www.candlewick.com

For Jordan and Chloe, my good-luck charms
M. M.

To my talented pal Megan McDonald
P. H. R.

Table of Contents

Judy Moody

Be-charmed
third-grade pig sitter;
Queen of the Growlery

Who's

Dad

Spelling-list rescuer

Mom

Road-trip mastermind

Stink

Prize Claw timekeeper
and fellow pig sitter

Who

Rocky

Best friend and
#1 study buddy

Frank

Floater in the Moater
bowler buddy

PeeGee Wee Gee the Pig

This little piggy went to D.C.

Jessica

*Very berry cherry funny
money* super speller

The Lucky Penny

She, Judy Moody, had a penny. Not just any penny. Not a regular old Abe Lincoln penny.

A lucky penny. No lie!

Judy and her family took Grandma Lou out to breakfast at the Two Chicks on a Raft Diner. Stink ordered—what else?—silver-dollar pancakes. Judy said, "I'll have the special—two chicks on a raft. And some moo juice."

"Moo juice?" asked Stink, sitting up.

Judy pointed to all the funny names for food on the menu. "Two eggs on toast. And milk to drink."

"Chocolate moo for me, please," said Stink.

"So anyway," Judy told her family, "Grandma Lou took me roller-skating at Mount Trashmore, right?"

"And we rolled right past one of those penny machines," said Grandma Lou.

"And she gave me this way-old penny she had from the 1970s—"

"Waayy old," said Grandma Lou, smiling.

"And we put it in the machine and—check it out!" Judy held up a penny with a four-leaf clover

inside a horseshoe that said MY LUCKY PENNY. MT. TRASHMORE, VA.

"That's not a lucky penny," said Stink. "That's a squished penny. Weird. It looks like it got run over."

"It's still a lucky penny, Stink," said Judy. "Says so right on it, see?"

"How much did you pay for that?" Stink asked.

"Fifty-one cents," said Judy.

"Fifty-one cents! You paid fifty-one cents for a penny?"

"A *lucky* penny," said Judy.

"It's a special penny," said Mom. "A keepsake."

"A souvenir," said Dad.

"I'm so going to start collecting these,"

said Judy, rubbing her penny. "It'll be my new thing."

"I thought your new thing was collecting banana stickers," said Stink. "And Popsicle sticks with jokes on them."

"Stink? Do you have to know everything about me?"

"Kids," Dad warned. "Don't start."

While they waited for their food, Judy got an idea. She had seen a machine in the front lobby. A way-cool machine full of something else she collected. Stuffed animals!

"Grandma Lou?" Judy asked. "Do you have any quarters?"

Grandma Lou dug down to the bottom of her purse. "Four. Will that do?"

"Yes. Thanks, Grandma Lou!"

"Are you gonna smash quarters, too?" Stink asked.

"No, I just want to play the Super Claw," said Judy. She pointed to the glass case.

"Forget it," said Stink. "It's super-impossible. Nobody beats The Claw!"

"Yah-huh," said Judy. "People do. Or else the glass case would be full. Besides, it's fun to try. What's there to lose?"

"Duh! Money!"

Judy scooped up the quarters. "C'mon, Stink-o. Before the food gets here."

She dashed away from the table and headed for the lobby.

"Wait for me!" said Stink.

"One, two, three . . ." Judy said. "We have exactly four quarters."

"It costs a dollar a turn!" said Stink. "That's four quarters."

"I'll go first," said Judy.

"But then I get to go *never*," said Stink.

"Not if I win. If I win, we get a free turn," said Judy.

"Like I said. Never," said Stink.

"C'mon, Stink," said Judy, pressing her nose to the glass. "Which one should we go for?"

"The yellow elephant," said Stink. "His ear's sticking up. No wait. The blue monkey! No wait! The green lion."

"Purple rhino it is!" said Judy. *Clinkety-clink-clink-clink!* The four quarters landed in the machine. *Whirr!* The thirty seconds began ticking away. Judy grabbed the joystick. She moved the giant arm until the claw dangled right over the purple rhino.

"Hurry up!" said Stink, standing on tiptoes to see better. "You only have twenty-three more seconds."

She, Judy Moody, went in for the big grab.

Stink leaned in closer. "Six seconds!" he said.

The open tentacles of the claw came down around the rhino's snout. "Gotcha!" Judy whispered. She pressed the big green button on the joystick to lock the claw in place.

"Don't drop him!" shouted Stink.

Judy held her breath. She tried not to itch. She tried not to twitch. *Steady, steady. Careful, careful.* With the joystick, she eased the rhino over to the chute and *wa la!* She let go. He slid down the chute into the hatch.

Judy opened the prize door and pulled

out the purple rhino. "Mine, all mine!" she cooed, hugging it to her.

"Free turn," said Stink. "I'm next."

"No way, Stinker."

"But you said—"

"Stink, I won! I beat The Claw! I'm on a roll. Do you really want to mess with that kind of luck?"

Stink shook his head no.

Judy reached into her pocket and rubbed her lucky penny. "Ready?" she asked.

Stink nodded. "Ready, Freddy," he said.

Judy took hold of the joystick. Her hand was sweating. She took a deep breath.

"Orange cow," said Stink, pointing. "Go for the orange cow!"

In just under seventeen seconds, Judy managed to nab the orange cow, keep it in the grip of the claw, and send it down the chute to the prize door.

"We won," said Stink, reaching in first to grab the orange cow. "You did it. You beat The Claw two times in a row!"

"Free turn," said the machine. "Free turn."

"Should we go for three?" Judy asked.

"Yeah, yeah, yeah-yeah-yeah," said Stink. He was so excited his cheeks flushed bright red.

"Okay, Stinker. Your turn. The pressure is on."

"No way!" said Stink. "You're on a crazy good winning streak."

Judy took out her lucky penny and set it on the machine. "C'mon, lucky penny," she whispered. She clutched the joystick one more time.

This time, she grabbed a blue monkey—barely—by the tip of the tippy tail. She pulled back on the joystick, slowly, slowly.

"Don't drop it!" said Stink. "You're going to drop it."

Blue Monkey's head bumped into Pink Crab's claw!

"Watch out!" said Stink.

At last, Judy let go of the button and Blue Monkey dropped down into the prize chute. Music went off. Lights blinked and flashed. "Game o-ver!" said the machine.

Judy and Stink rushed back to their table, clutching Purple Rhino, Orange Cow, and Blue Monkey.

"Whoa," said Stink. "You beat The Claw three times in a row! That's like some kind of record."

Judy held up her shiny coin and smiled. "It's all because of my lucky penny, of course!" she said.

Good Luck x 3

The next day, three things happened to Judy. Three good-luck things.

Judy woke up just like she did on any other normal old day. She ran downstairs to eat breakfast just like she did on any other normal old day.

"Stink, pass the Lucky Os, please."

Stink passed the cereal. Judy poured Lucky Os into her bowl. She added milk.

That's when it happened. Good-Luck Thing Number One.

One, two, three, four, five, six, seven fun-shaped marshmallows floated in her cereal. "Stink! Check it out! How many marshmallows do you see?"

Stink counted. "Seven?"

"Exactly! Seven is a lucky number. In fact, seven is the luckiest number of all."

"Can I eat a lucky marshmallow?" Stink reached his spoon toward her bowl.

Judy swatted his hand away. "No! I have to see if any of these are purple horseshoes. Horseshoes are super lucky."

Judy reached in and plucked out a purple horseshoe. "It's a double!" she squealed. "Two purple horseshoes stuck together. Double stuff is lucky, too."

Stink looked in his bowl. He looked

in the box. But he did not see any more double lucky marshmallows. "You have all the luck," said Stink.

He put a spoonful of un-lucky cereal in his mouth. He slumped down in his chair to chew. Suddenly, his eyes stopped blinking and his whole body froze.

"What? What's wrong?" Judy asked.

"My lucky ketchup packet!" said Stink, with a mouthful of half-chewed cereal. "I sat on it!"

"Huh?"

"Yesterday at the diner, when you had a lucky penny in your pocket, I wanted a lucky thing, too. So I put a ketchup packet in my back pocket for *my* lucky thing.

But I forgot about it and I think I just smooshed it." Stink made a scrunched-up, I-just-sat-on-ketchup face.

"Ooh, ick. Let me see!" said Judy.

Stink stood up and wiped at his pants with his hands. Sure enough, there was ketchup smeared all over his pants. There was ketchup smooshed all over the chair.

Judy handed Stink a dish towel. "Here, wipe up the ketchup volcano."

She closed up the cereal box. Ouch! Paper cut! (Bad luck.) But a paper cut meant she got to wear a Band-Aid! (Good luck.)

Judy ran upstairs and took out her Crazy Strips collection. She had eyeball bandages, zombies, and crime-scene tape ones. Rainbows, sushi, nesting dolls. Toast!

She shook out all the toast-shaped bandages and wrapped one around her finger. Wait just a peanut-butter-and-jelly minute! What's this? A folded-up wad of . . . dollar bills!

Ten whole dollars! What were they doing in the box of Crazy Strips? Maybe Stink hid them and forgot about them.

Who cares! She was rich!

Judy origami-folded each dollar bill into a ring. A money ring! One for each finger. Good-Luck Thing Number Two.

☙   ☙   ☙

That afternoon, Judy Moody, Blue Monkey, Purple Rhino, and ten lucky dollars got dropped off at Jessica Finch's birthday bowling party at Starlight Lanes. When she got inside, she raced around the lobby looking for a Super Claw machine.

"Are you looking for us?" asked Frank and Rocky, coming up beside her. Frank pointed to a lane in the far corner where the Finches were bowling. Jessica Finch waved. "We're over there."

"First I was looking for a Super Claw machine," Judy told her friends. She showed them Purple Rhino and Blue Monkey. She told them about her good-luck streak. She held out her hands. Each finger had a money ring. Ten dollars =

ten tries to beat the Super Claw! "I could win ten tons of stuffed animals."

Rocky and Frank raced around after her, looking too.

"No Super Claw machine," said Rocky.

"No Super Claw machine," said Frank.

Bummeroo.

Jessica Finch ran up to them. "Hi, Judy! Can you believe I get a bowling party for my birthday? C'mon, guys! The Xtreme Bowling Challenge is about to begin!" The kids rushed back to the far lane.

"Hi Mr. and Mrs. Finch," said Judy.

"Hey, kiddo," said Mr. Finch. "Glad you could make it."

"Love your bowling-pin pajama bottoms," said Mrs. Finch, smiling.

"Thanks!" said Judy.

All of a sudden, the lights went down. Music came over the loudspeakers. Neon-bright colored lights flickered and flashed on the bowling lanes.

"Rare!" said Judy.

A voice came over the sound system. "It's time—Xtreme Bowling time—for people who like to knock stuff down!"

Everybody cheered.

"As you know, each bowler gets three balls. And the goal is to get not one, not two, but three strikes in a row."

"Whoa," said Frank.

A guy dressed as a bowling pin came over to their lane. "Are you, Birthday Girl

Jessica Finch, ready to rock the Xtreme Challenge?" he yelled into the mike.

"Yes!" she screamed.

"Let's get this par-tee star-ted!" said the human bowling pin.

Other bowlers gathered around to watch. "Go, Jessica!" everybody yelled.

Jessica Finch rolled her first ball down

the lane. "Baby Ball!" said the human bowling pin. He used funny names like Big Ears and Snake Eyes for bowling moves.

"Try again," the guy said. Jessica rolled the second ball.

"Powder Puff! Sorry. Not hard enough. Once more for the B-day girl."

Jessica rolled a third ball.

"A 3-6-10 split. That's what we call a Poison Ivy. Not bad, but sorry, no cigar."

Rocky took the Xtreme Challenge next.

"Will he choke?" asked the human bowling pin. Rocky's first ball hit three pins. His second ball hit five pins. On Rocky's third try, the guy yelled, "Blowout! All but one. So close."

Frank Pearl took the Xtreme Challenge next.

"Try Number One. Creeper! Try Number Two. Sleeper! Try Number Three. Floater in the Moater! That means gutter ball, folks. Next!"

At last it was Judy's turn. She stepped up to the lane. She rubbed her lucky penny. She rubbed the bowling ball. She held it in front of her, lining it up. She squinted one eye, pulled back her arm, and let it fly.

"Lookin' good, lookin' good, lookin'— STEE-rike!" yelled the human bowling pin. "We have a winner! But can she do it again?"

Judy bowled a second ball.

"Double-double! Super strike!" yelled the guy. "This one's on a lucky streak. Can the girl in the I ATE A SHARK shirt make it three in a row? Or will it be a dead apple in the gutter?"

Judy bowled a third ball. It leaned left. It leaned right. It picked up speed, straightened up, and *KA-BOOM!* All ten pins toppled like a house of sugar packets.

Neon lights flashed. A horn blared. Everybody crowded around went cuckoo.

"And we have a Turkey!" yelled the guy.

"A Turkey? But I knocked down all the pins!" said Judy. Mr. and Mrs. Finch laughed.

"A turkey means *three* strikes in a row!"

The human bowling pin took Judy's arm and held it in the air like a prizefighter. "Didn't this girl just BOWL you over, folks?" The crowd went wild. The human bowling pin bobbed his head in a turkey dance. "Gobble, gobble, gobble." The human bowling pin turned a cartwheel across three lanes. "Congrats, Shark Girl. Your name goes on the Bowling Pin Wall of Fame."

"Wow!" said Jessica.

"Double wow!" said Rocky.

"Triple wow!" said Frank.

"That was really something," said Mrs. Finch.

"Glow sticks for everyone at the birthday girl's party!" said the guy. "And

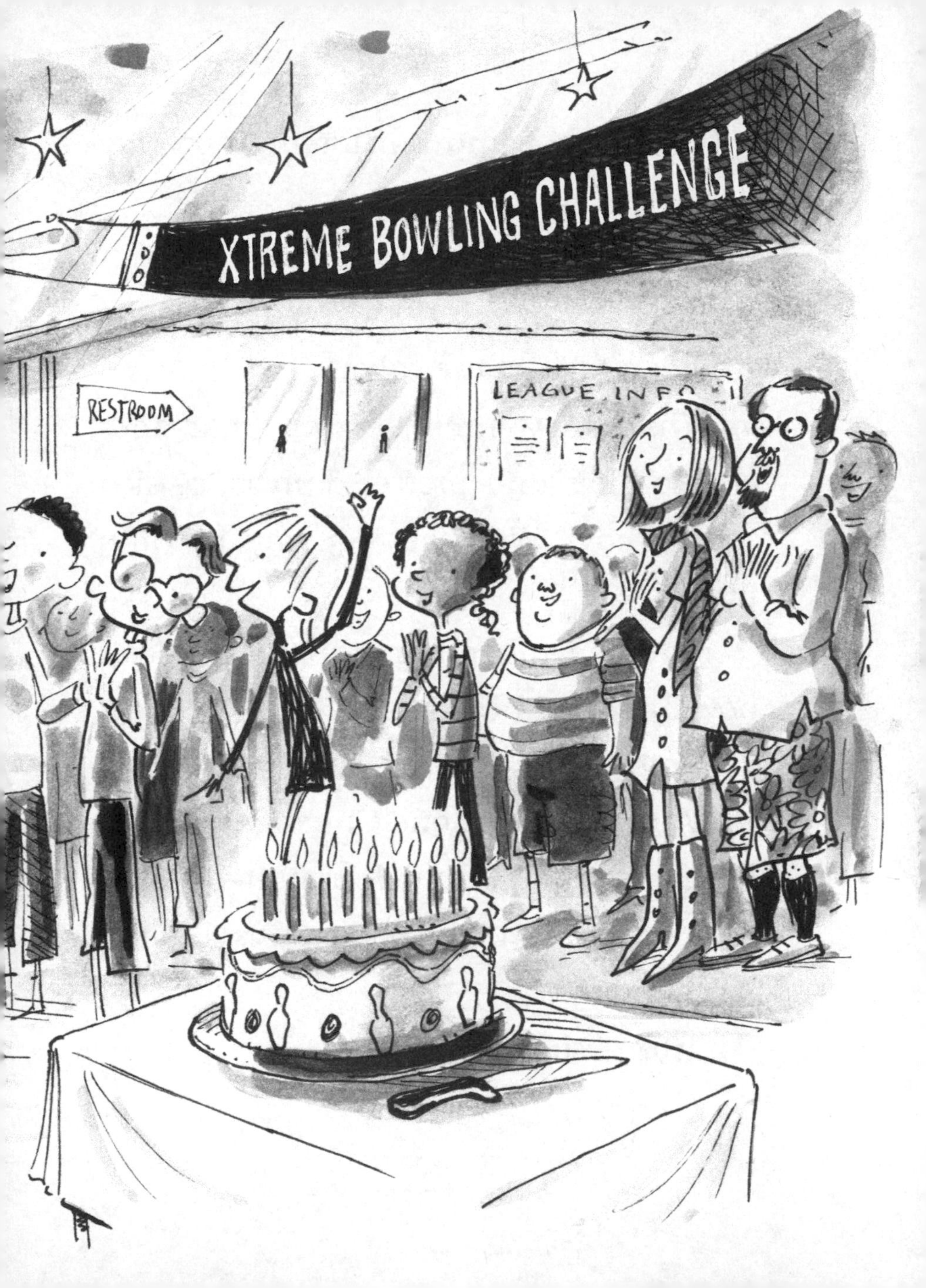
XTREME BOWLING CHALLENGE
RESTROOM
LEAGUE INFO

a blow-up bowling pin for the birthday girl!"

"Thanks!" said Jessica.

"Let's get those birthday treats up here. And don't forget the cake!"

While they munched on mac-and-cheese bites and pretzel dippers, Jessica said, "Judy? Will you sign my bowling pin?"

Judy signed her autograph on Jessica's bowling pin. In cursive.

"You sure are lucky," said Jessica.

"All we got was one Christmas Tree, a Poison Ivy, and a bunch of gutter balls," said Frank. "I mean Poodle Puffs. I mean Powder Puffs."

"Huh?" said Rocky.

"Whatever. You know. Funny names, like the bowling pin guy uses. Poison Ivy is a 3-6-10 split. And Christmas Tree is a 3-7-10 split."

"I owe it all to my lucky penny," said Judy. She held it up and kissed it.

"*Lucky* is your middle name," said Frank.

"Just call me Judy 'Lucky' Moody," said Judy.

Planet Lucky

At inside recess on Monday morning, Frank asked Judy, "Do you think something lucky will happen to you at school today?"

"Sure. Why not?" said Judy.

"Like what?" asked Rocky.

"Like . . . maybe I'll find my missing *Clue of the Broken Locket* library book or

Frank will give me back my Grouchy pencil."

"Oops," said Frank, fishing around inside his desk.

"Or I'll get picked to take Peanut home this weekend. Or Mr. Todd will cancel our spelling test."

"Yeah, right," said Rocky. "The only thing that would cancel a spelling test is if lightning struck the school, it caught on fire, and we all had to run out of the building."

Just then, Mr. Todd blinked the lights. "Settle down, class. Let's get back to work."

Mr. Todd leaned against his desk. "Instead of a spelling test today—"

"I knew it!" Judy blurted.

"Whoa. This *is* your lucky day!" whispered Frank.

"Excuse me?" said Mr. Todd. "Am I going to have to get out the Interrupting Jar again?"

"Sorry," said Judy, zipping her lips.

"As I was saying, instead of a spelling test today, we're going to have a practice spelling bee. As you all know, our class spelling bee is coming up in a week. Whoever wins will get to go with the winners from the other third-grade classes at Virginia Dare School to take part in the Great Third Grade Spelling Bee at the end of the month."

"Everybody knows Jessica Finch is the WBS," said Judy.

"WBS?" said Mr. Todd, wrinkling his forehead.

"World's Best Speller," said Judy.

"You never know," said Mr. Todd. "If you try hard enough, you could be the lucky speller who gets to represent Class 3T in Washington, D.C."

Washington, D.C.! As in home of the president and the Museum of Doctor Stuff and the giant giant's head sticking up out of the ground? As in the same exact place where Stink got to go to the White House and she didn't?

She, Judy Moody, could not believe her lucky-ducky ears. She could not bite her un-interrupting tongue for one more second.

Judy raised her hand. "Excuse me, Mr. Todd. Did you say Washington, D.C.?"

"Yes," said Mr. Todd. "The Great Third-Grade Spelling Bee will be held at our sister school, Orchard Elementary, in Washington, D.C."

"Did you know that's where the White House is?" Judy asked.

"I am aware of that, yes," said Mr. Todd, smiling.

"Well, did you know they also have the Museum of Doctor Stuff with a for-real Abraham Lincoln bone?"

"I did not know that," said Mr. Todd. "Very interesting."

"It is," said Judy. "They have an actual hunk of his skull. No lie."

"Ooh! Gross!" said the other kids in the class.

"Who knows? Maybe you'll get a

chance to see it." Mr. Todd stood up and rubbed his hands together. "Okay, Class 3T. Are you ready for our practice bee? All the words are from the study sheets you've been working on these last few weeks. When I call your name, please come up front and face the class. Spell your word and use it in a sentence, please."

Judy Moody could not keep her mind on spelling. All she could think about was how much she wanted to go to Washington, D.C. D.C. was for Definitely Cool!

If only she didn't have to *spell* to get there.

Then Judy remembered. She, Judy Moody, had her lucky penny.

Frank spelled *measles* with a *Z*. Rocky spelled *quesadilla,* but he forgot about the *L*s and said *Y* instead. And Jessica "A-is-for-Aardwolf" Finch spelled *bonanza.* Perfectly. *Z* and all.

Judy would rather get *measles* than have to spell *quesadilla* in a spelling *bonanza.*

Finally, Mr. Todd called on Judy. She took one last look at her study sheet before getting up. Her feet felt like *cement.* Her stomach turned a *somersault.* If only she could write spelling words in *graffiti* on her hand.

That would get her nowhere but the *principal's* office.

Judy stood in front of the class. Her

hands started to sweat. She reached into her pocket and rubbed her lucky penny.

Please give me a lucky word, she thought to herself. *An easy-peasy word from page one of the study pages, like* berry *or* cherry *or* funny *or* bunny.

"Judy," said Mr. Todd. "The word is *punctuate.*"

Punk-chew-ate! *Punctuate* was not a lucky word. *Punctuate* was not an easy-peasy page-one word. *Punctuate* was not *berry* or *cherry* or *funny* or *bunny*! Judy felt a lump in her throat. Her mouth went bone-dry as a desert. She felt cactus prickles up and down her arms.

Maybe she was coming down with a *measles bonanza.*

She looked around the room for help. Posters lined the bulletin board. Posters for grammar, spelling, and . . . punctuation!

Holy Macaroni! This was her lucky day after all. *Punctuate* was part of *punctuation.* All she had to do was remember to end with an e.

"*Punctuate.*   P-U-N-C-T-U-A-T-um-E! *Punctuate.*" She let out a whoosh of air.

"Can you use it in a sentence?" asked Mr. Todd.

"I'd like to punctuate the person who thought up spelling bees," said Judy.

Class 3T cracked up.

Mr. Todd rolled his eyes to the ceiling.

"I think we'll have to punctuate this spelling bee until tomorrow." He turned to erase the board. "Don't forget to take your study packets home, class. Pair up with a study buddy and practice, practice, practice. Our class spelling bee is in one week."

"Wowzer, Judy!" said Frank as soon as the final bell rang. "How did you know how to spell that hard word?"

"Pure luck," said Rocky. "It was right there on the bulletin board, huh Judy? I saw you see it."

"For real? I didn't even see you see me see it!" said Judy.

"You're like the luckiest person on the planet or something," said Frank.

Judy did not even say "Or something." She *was* the luckiest person ever. There was no stopping her now.

"Bye, Mr. Todd," Judy said on her way out the door. "See you in Washington, D.C."

"Keep up that positive attitude, Judy. I've always said you can do anything you set your mind to. Even spelling."

Judy smiled a secret smile to herself. Mr. Todd did not know that she, Judy Moody, was on a lucky streak. And she planned to ride that lucky streak all the way to Washington, D.C.

The Bad-Luck Charm

It was one week, two study buddies (Rocky plus Frank), and three practice bees later.

Judy Moody shook her Magic 8 Ball.

"Will I win the class spelling bee?"

Reply hazy.

"Will I finally get to go to Washington, D.C.?"

Ask again later.

Double drat!

"Judy?" said Dad. "Your class bee is

tomorrow, isn't it? Are you up to speed on all your spelling words?"

"*Berry, furry, merry, hurry, cherry, bunny, funny,*" said Judy.

"We mean *past* page one of your spelling packet," said Mom.

Hello! Judy reached into her pocket and pulled out her lucky penny. She held it up for Mom and Dad to see.

Mom came over and put an arm around her shoulder. "Honey, I know how much you like that lucky penny. And it's fine to carry it around—for fun."

"But if you're serious about winning a spelling bee," said Dad, "you're going to have to work at it."

Mom nodded. "You're not going to

win the spelling bee based on *one* lucky penny."

"In fact—" began Dad, but Judy did not want to hear it. She clomped upstairs to study before Mom and Dad could say any more bad stuff about good luck.

She took out her spelling list. She turned to the hard page. As in D-I-F-F-I-C-U-L-T.

Destiny. She closed her eyes. Des+tiny. D-E-S-T-I-N-Y. It was her own tiny *destiny* to go to Washington, D.C.

So far so good. Next word. *Present.* She closed her eyes again. P-R-E-S-I-D-E-N-T. The *president* lived in Washington, D.C. Just think. If she, Judy Moody, was lucky enough to go to D.C., she just-might-maybe see the *president* himself.

Judy opened her eyes and stared at the word *present*-not-*president*. She'd practiced the wrong word. It was no use.

She got out a fake-fur neon-pink rabbit's-foot keychain, three acorns, two cat's-eye marbles, and one lucky stone. Seven more lucky charms!

Her mother was probably right. *One*

lucky penny was *not* enough to win a
spelling bee. She would fill the pockets
of her cargo pants with tons of good-luck
charms. Good luck times seven!

Judy went to sleep sure that good luck
was her *destiny* for the *present.*

Until . . . the next day.

Spelling Bee day!

On the bus, Judy reached into her right
shorts pocket. Empty! Of all days to over-
sleep. How could she forget to wear her

pants full of lucky charms? Seven extra-sure foolproof lucky charms were in the pockets of her cargo pants—at home on her bottom bunk. Bringing good luck to nobody, except maybe Mouse the cat.

She reached into her left pocket. Phew! Good thing she still had her lucky penny. All was not lost.

"Third-graders!" said Mr. Todd when Judy got to school. "Are you ready?"

"Yes!"

"What are you ready for?"

"Spelling Bee!"

"Put away your study folders and form a line at the back of the room," said Mr. Todd. "May the best speller win!"

Judy put her spelling folder away. She

never did make it past the first few words on the hard page.

All of a sudden, she did not feel so good. She was in a cherry-berry hurry-flurry to get out of the room.

"Mr. Todd, may I please go to the rest-room?" Judy asked.

"Quickly," said Mr. Todd.

Judy speed-walked down the hall to the girl's bathroom. She did not really have to go, but she sat down on the toilet. She hummed "Twinkle, Twinkle, Little Star" to calm herself down. She recited "Tikki tikki tembo-no sa rembo-chari bari ruchi-pip peri pembo" from a story her dad used to tell her about a kid with a very long name.

Judy did not know how many minutes went by. But if she stayed away much longer, Mr. Todd would send somebody to find her.

On the way back to class, she reached into her pocket to rub her lucky penny.

Holy Macaroni!

Her left pocket was empty! The lucky penny was G-O-N-E *gone*!

Judy rushed back to the girl's room. She looked around the sink. She looked on the floor. She looked you-know-where.

There, in all its copper coolness, was her lucky penny. *In the toilet!*

The upside-down horseshoe smiled up at her.

She did not have a ruler. She did not

have a grouchy pencil. She did not have anything to fish it out with. She, Judy Moody, stuck her real-not-fake hand in the toilet! C-O-L-D *cold!* G-R-O-S-S *gross!* Yuck and double-bluck.

She fished out the lucky penny.

Judy ran to the sink and washed off the

lucky penny. With soap. Double phew! That was a close one.

Back in Room 3T, the spell-a-thon was in full swing. Judy slid into line.

Jessica Finch got the word *bamboo*. No fair! Easy-peasy. Rocky got *caboose*. Double easy-peasy. Frank got *waffle*. His favorite food!

At last it was Judy's turn. Her heart beat faster. She double-crossed her fingers and squeezed her eyes shut. *Easy word, easy word,* she wished on her lucky penny.

"The word is *Chihuahua,*" said Mr. Todd.

Holy Burrito!

Judy opened her eyes. *Chi-wa-wa!* That was a way-hard word. A hard word that was not *bunny* or *funny*. A NOT page-one word.

She tried to picture the word. But all she could see were pugs. Not one Chihuahua. Maybe if she started spelling, she'd get lucky.

Judy cleared her throat. "C-H-I . . ." *Yikes. What came next?* "H - A - W - A - I - I. *Chihuahua*."

"Sorry," said Mr. Todd. "Incorrect. But you did spell *Hawaii* nicely."

What? Judy was dumbstruck. Her feet were frozen to her spot on the floor. This could not be happening. Judy was O-U-T *out* on the first word?

"Thank you, Judy," said Mr. Todd. "You may take your seat."

Judy sat down. She slumped in her chair. What in the world made her spell Hawaii? Had her lucky penny gone for-sure-and-absolute C-U-C-K-O-O?

For the rest of the spellathon, the room was a tornado of whirling, swirling words: *Mermaid. Butterscotch. Tornado.*

But Judy Moody did not seem to hear. Or see. Or notice.

Finally . . . Jessica Finch was the only one left standing. What an aardwolf.

"And the winner is Jessica Finch!" said Mr. Todd. "Congratulations, Jessica. You will be representing Class 3T in the Great Third-Grade Spelling Bee in Washington, D.C."

Everybody whooped and clapped. Judy

clapped, too. But she was not clapping on the inside.

Of all the luck! She, Judy Moody, would not be going to Washington, D.C. Her chances of visiting the District of Cool had just gone Down the Can. As in *toilet*.

Toilet! Of course! Her lucky penny. It must have gone kerflooey when she dropped it in the toilet. The toilet messed up its magic, jinxing her double-bad. Judy took the penny from her pocket. The smiling horseshoe had become an upside-down frown. ROAR!

Good-bye, good-luck penny. Hello, bad-luck charm.

Uck Bluck Luck

As soon as Judy got home, she looked for a place to hide her P.U. un-lucky penny. She zoomed around the house. Where-o-where? Stink's room! Stink liked smelly stuff, and he was not afraid of cooties.

She looked all around. Under Stink's pillow. Perfecto! Good riddance to bad luck.

Cheese Louise. Now she had NO luck

at all. If she was going to keep her good luck streak going, she needed a brand-new, un-P.U. good-luck charm for sure.

Judy grabbed the magnifying glass from her detective kit. She ran outside. Crawling on all fours, she peered closely at the grass, searching for a four-leaf clover for what felt like an hour. Or longer.

All of a sudden, the back door banged. "Whatcha doing?" Stink asked.

"Something," she said without looking up.

"Something what?" Stink asked, nose-to-nose with the grass now, too.

"I'm looking for good luck," said Judy, still not looking up.

"I had some good luck. Just now," said

Stink. He blew a bubble-gum bubble and popped it. "I found three whole pieces of Yubba Dubba gum in my desk that I didn't even know I had. Lucky, huh? The fortune in the comic says *You will soon take a trip.*"

Judy looked up. A trip! As in Washington, D.C.? If only *she* had gotten that fortune. No such luck. She went back to her search.

"Is that lucky grass or something?" Stink asked.

"Or something. If you must know, Stinker, I'm looking for a lucky four-leaf clover." So far she had found one rock, three dandelions, and about ten-hundred un-lucky three-leaf clovers. Not one single clover with four leaves.

Not even a lucky ladybug.

"Did you know the odds of finding a four-leaf clover are like ten-thousand to one? That means you have to look through nine-thousand nine-hundred and ninety-nine three-leaf clovers to find one."

"Thanks a lot," said Judy.

"It's possible," said Stink. "A guy in Alaska found 111,060 four-leaf clovers."

"Maybe I should move to Alaska," said Judy.

Just then, something landed on Stink's arm. "Hey, a ladybug!" said Stink. "Aren't they good luck?"

Judy popped up. "Just my luck. A ladybug landed on *you*!"

"Cool! *Three* lucky things have happened to me since I got home from school," said Stink. "I found that bubble gum I didn't know I had. And now this ladybug landed on me."

"That's two things. What's the third thing?"

"The third thing was really the first thing, which is why the second and third things must have happened."

"Is this a riddle?" Judy asked.

"Look what I found under my pillow." Stink held up the lucky penny. "And I didn't even lose a tooth! It's *my* lucky penny now. That's the third lucky thing that was really the first lucky thing."

Yikes. Maybe Judy had ditched the penny too soon. "Fine. But just so you know . . . it's a *bad*-luck penny now."

"Is not!" Stink held it right up to his face and planted a kiss on it. "Mine o mine o mine!" he sang.

"GROSS!" yelled Judy, making an ucky-blucky face.

"What?"

"Oh, nothing," said Judy.

Stink eyed the penny suspiciously now. "Tell me."

"It's just that—the penny has cooties."

"You're just saying that," said Stink.

"Stink, do you want to know *why* it's a bad-luck penny with cooties now? Because something happened that changed the good luck to bad."

"What?"

"It went plop. It did a high-dive belly

flop. Whooo . . . PSSH!" Judy mimed a high dive with her hand.

"Huh?"

"The toilet, Stink. I dropped it *in the toilet!*"

"UCCCKKK! Bluck, bluck, bluck, bluck, BLUCK!" Stink let go of the penny. It flew through the air and plopped in the grass. Judy made note of where it landed.

"Good riddance to bad cooties," said Stink. "You can be in that T. P. Club all by yourself. The Toilet Penny Club."

"Ha, ha, very funny, Stink," said Judy.

Stink ran inside the house. Judy crawled across the grass and plucked the penny from the crabgrass, smiling as if she'd just picked a four-leaf clover.

She did NOT kiss the penny. She put it back in her pocket.

Just then Mom called, "Judy, can you come inside for a sec?"

Judy ran into the kitchen. Dad stood at the sink, doing dishes. Stink was eating frozen corn from a freezer bag. "What's up?"

"Mrs. Finch, you know, Jessica's mother, just called."

"Uh-huh."

"You know that Jessica is going to D.C. for the third-grade spelling bee?"

"Uh-huh."

"And you know that she just got a pot-bellied pig for her birthday?"

"Uh-huh. PeeGee WeeGee. "

"Well, Jessica would like to know if you can take care of PeeGee WeeGee while she's at the spelling bee?"

Jessica Finch, Super Speller, was going to Washington, D.C., District of Cooties. She, Judy Moody, would be stuck in Frog Neck Un-lucky Lake, Virginia, being a great big pig sitter. *Oink!*

That little piggy went to D.C. This little piggy stayed home. . . . This little piggy went roar, roar, roar all the way home.

"I don't know," said Judy.

Dad wiped his hands on the towel. "Mom and I thought you'd jump at the chance to go to Washington, D.C."

"Washington what? Who? Huh? Me?" Judy asked, looking from Mom to Dad.

Mom laughed. "Jessica doesn't want to leave her pig behind, since she just got him and all, so they found a pet-friendly hotel. They're taking PeeGee with them."

"But they need a pig sitter when they're at the spelling bee. So, Mom and I thought we might take you and Stink down a day early and do a little sightseeing first," said Dad.

"For real?"

Holy Baloney! Judy Moody could not believe her this-little-piggy ears.

"So my bubble-gum fortune came true?" Stink bounced up and down on his toes. "I *am* going to take a trip soon!"

Bubble gum, schmubble gum. This could mean only one thing: Judy's lucky penny still had some luck in it! Good thing she rescued it from Stink.

The Moodys were going to the District of (Not) Cooties.

"So . . . what do you think?" Mom asked. "What should I tell Mrs. Finch?"

"Tell her I said, 'Judy Moody, Pig Sitter, at your service!'"

The District of Cool

Road trip! The Moodys were on their way to Washington, D.C. Double Cool!

In the car, Judy could hardly sit still. In almost exactly one hour and twenty-seven minutes, she would be in the District of (not) Cooties!

Except it took more like four hours because of Stink.

1.) He had stop to go to the bathroom.

2.) He had to stop to buy some Yubba Dubba bubble gum.

3.) He saw a giant statue of a giant's head coming up out of the ground and—*POP!*—got bubble gum all over his face and hair.

4.) He had to stop to get de-gummed.

When at last, finally, the end, they got there, Judy had to wake him up. "Stink! We're here! The District of Coolsville!"

Dad parked and they walked along the Mall that was not a mall at all. It was more like a park with a long reflecting pool and tons of famous, cool stuff you see on money. Judy saw the fancy White House where the Big Boss of the Whole

Entire Country lived. Aka the Prez. Plus the First Lady and First Kids and First Dog.

Da-da-da Dome! Judy saw a big important building with a dome where some Big Important People decided Big Important Stuff like laws or something.

Judy saw a tall, skinny pyramid thingie called the Washington Monument. Mom said it was almost as tall as the Eiffel Tower!

Her eyes bugged out when she saw the real, actual statue of Abe Lincoln, called the Lincoln Memorial, just like on the back of a not-lucky penny. RARE!

"I bet James Madison, best-president-ever, stood right here," said Stink. "James Madison could have spit on this sidewalk.

James Madison could have eaten a hot dog on this bench."

"Hot dogs weren't even invented yet," said Judy.

"How do you know?" said Stink.

"I know you have James Madison on the brain," said Judy.

Dad checked his watch. "Who wants to go to the museum?"

"Is it the boring kind? Or the way-not-boring kind?" said Judy.

"Way-not-boring," said Mom, pointing to a bunch of museums that were part of the Smithsonian.

"Whoa! Check it out," Stink said, running down the sidewalk. "A castle!"

"Let's start there," said Dad. "It's the info center."

"What do they have at this way-not-boring museum?" Judy asked.

"The Hope Diamond," said Mom.

"Lincoln's stovepipe hat," said Dad.

"Shrunken heads and dino poop!" said Stink.

"They do not," said Judy.

"Yah-huh. No lie," said Stink. "I saw it when I came here before with my class. Plus they have three thousand sea slugs, fifty thousand flies, and one hundred and fifteen thousand bird eggs."

"We are SO there," said Judy.

Here is what she, Judy Moody, saw up-close-and-personal at the way-not-boring museum:

- Astronaut boots
- Barf bags
- Brick from the Great Wall of China
- Robber crabs (They steal forks and spoons! No lie!)
- 7 million beetles, including the endangered Northeast beach tiger beetle
- 1 million samples of dirt
- 10,000-year-old sloth dung
- President Warren G. Harding's pajamas
- Lock of George Washington's hair (+ hairy locks of 15 more presidents)
- Way-old pack of gum

        ☺   ☺   ☺

After the museum, they hit the gift shop.

DIRT

BARF
BAG

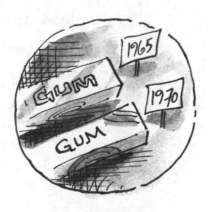

GUM 1965

GUM 1970

Judy used her lucky Crazy Strips money to get freeze-dried ice cream (just like the astronauts). And a book about stuff to make with duct tape.

Stink already had the James Madison six-inch ruler, the James Madison mini statue, and the James Madison friendship coin. And they were all sold out of James Madison talking bobbleheads. So he got a plastic un-talking statue of Abe Lincoln.

"Abe Lincoln is my second-best president," said Stink as they walked back to the car. "See? It says eman-ci-potato at the bottom."

"Potato? Let me see," said

Judy. She sounded out the word at the bottom.

"E-M-A-N-C-I-P-A-T-I-O-N. What's *emancipation?*" Judy asked Mom and Dad.

"It means to set free," said Mom.

"Lincoln set potatoes free?" Stink asked.

Mom chuckled. "No, Lincoln is famous for writing something called the Emancipation Proclamation."

"In it, he said slaves should be free," Dad added.

"Everybody knows that," said Stink.

"Speaking of Abe Lincoln," said Judy.

"Will we have time to go to the Museum of Doctor Stuff? They have Abe Lincoln's skull bone there. No lie."

"Sorry, Jelly Bean," said Dad. "Mom already checked. The National Museum of Health and Medicine had a power outage. They're closed today."

"Rat fink," said Judy.

"How about the World's Almost-Biggest Chair?" Stink asked. "I didn't get to see that last time. Can we go? Can we? Can we?"

"Sure," said Dad.

"No fair. Stink gets to do his thing and my thing is closed. That stinks on ice."

"Tell you what," said Mom, checking

her map. "We can drive past the chair on our way to the Frederick Douglass House in Cedar Hill."

"Frederick Douglass! Mr. Todd told us all about him for Black History Month."

"I thought you might like that," said Mom.

"Who's Frederick Douglass?" Stink asked.

"He was a great American thinker and speaker," said Dad.

"He was a slave and he escaped and fought for freedom," said Mom.

"He told President Lincoln how being a slave was really, really bad," said Judy. "And he said everybody should be able to vote. He even got in a fight with Lincoln about it. But that was like four score and seven million years ago."

Mom smiled.

"I think Mr. Todd would be proud of you," said Dad.

"And now I can tell him I saw his house!"

❧   ❧   ❧

The World's Almost-Biggest Chair sat out on the sidewalk in front of a parking lot.

"Can I climb up it?" Stink asked.

"Go ahead," said Judy. "If you want to get the World's Biggest Time-Out!"

Next stop: Cedar Hill. When they got to the Frederick Douglass house, there was an orange plastic fence around it, and yellow tape that said DO NOT CROSS.

"Under construction," said Mom.

"Aw, this is closed, too?" Judy asked. Double rat fink! She should have rubbed her lucky penny.

A park ranger came out and said they

were fixing up the house, and all the stuff was in storage. But they could take a tour of the grounds.

Bor-ing! Judy and Stink sat on a bummed-out bench while Mom and Dad walked around and read blah-blah-blah to each other from their guidebooks.

The flyer with the map had a lot of pictures. "Here, I'll give you the tour, Stink," said Judy. "This is a fancy bedroom. This is a fancy room where he played checkers. This is the not-so-fancy kitchen."

Stink peered at the shiny pictures. "Hey, wait. What's this?" Judy saw a picture of a little stone house with a chimney. "Stink! Follow me!"

Judy led the way to a little stone house

in the backyard. Inside was a high desk with a stool. "What is it?" Stink asked as they stepped through the doorway.

"It's called the Growlery," said Judy. "This is where Frederick Douglass came to growl when he was in a bad mood."

"No. What is it for real?"

"That *is* for real, Stink. No lie. It says so right here." Judy pointed to the caption under the picture. "He had a whole house for bad moods."

"A bad mood house. Whoa," said Stink. "GRRRRRRR!" He roared like a lion.

"ROARRRRRRR!" said Judy.

Mom and Dad poked their heads into the Growlery.

"It's a house for bad moods!" said Judy.

"I see," said Dad.

"I heard," said Mom.

"We should move this to our house. For Judy!" Stink cracked himself up.

"Time to go, kids," said Dad. "We have to meet the Finches for dinner so Judy can find out about taking care of PeeGee. Then we'll check into our hotel."

"Can't we stay a little longer?" asked Stink.

"Please-pretty-please with astronaut ice cream on top?" Judy asked.

"Five minutes," said Mom.

❦   ❦   ❦

She, Judy Moody, was still the luckiest kid alive. How many kids got to go to the District of Cool and see a giant giant's head, robber crabs, and a 10,000-year-old ball of dung. And scream their heads off in a Bad Mood house. All in one day! Washington was Washing*fun!*

Finch-Face Freakout

Dinnertime! The Moodys waited for Jessica Finch and her family at KaBob's Place.

Stink showed Judy the menu. "Every food here is on a stick. Hot-dog kabobs. Batter-dipped-veggie kabobs. Even fruit kabobs."

Judy was building the Washington Monument out of sugar packets. "Stink, don't shake the—Tim-ber!" said Judy, as her sugar packets came crashing down.

At last, the Finches arrived. Judy and Stink could not stop talking about Washingfun. They told Jessica about the Bad Mood House and the giant chair and the way-old dung.

Judy glanced all around. "Hey, where's your pig?" she asked.

"PeeGee WeeGee's in the car," said Jessica.

"He'll be okay in his kennel while we eat," said Mr. Finch.

After they ordered, Mom said, "So, tomorrow's the big spelling bee, Jessica. How do you feel?"

"My tummy's doing gymnastics," said Jessica. "It's like the Olympics in there."

"Nothing a grilled-cheese kabob won't fix," said Mrs. Finch.

"I could never ever spell in front of a million people," said Judy. "Even *with* my lucky penny."

Jessica Finch took out her list of spelling words. "I have to keep studying. Only seventeen hours and thirty-three minutes till Bee Time."

"Hey. Want me to quiz you?" Judy asked. "I'll be your study buddy."

"Great idea, girls," said Mom.

Judy ran her finger down the list. Jessica spelled *neighbor* and *zipper* and *alligator*. She spelled *library* and *geography*.

"Spell *shampoo banana*," said Stink.

"*Shampoo banana* is not on the spelling list, Stink."

"S-H-A-M-P-O-O B-A-N-A-N-A," said Jessica.

"Sure," said Judy, "but can you spell *berryfurrymerrycherryhoneybunnyfunny?*"

"That's like half the words on page one," Jessica said.

"I bet you can, Sweet Pea," said Mr. Finch.

Jessica took a deep breath. "B-E-R-R-Y-F-U-R-R-Y-M-E-R-R-Y-C-H-E-R-R-Y-H-O-N-E-Y-B-U-N-N-Y-F-U-N-N-Y."

"As your study buddy," said Judy, "Can I just say? You are *so* going to win."

"We heard Orchard Elementary has a boy named Sanjay Sharma who's really good. He may be tough to beat," said Mr. Finch.

"Yes, but can he spell half the words on page one at warp speed without taking a breath?"

"Thanks," said Jessica.

At the salad bar, Jessica spelled *mushroom* and *watermelon*. She spelled *artichoke, cucumber,* and *cauliflower.*

"Even the salad is on a stick!" said Jessica, showing off her plate.

"Jessica can spell the whole salad bar!" Judy told everybody at the table. She set the spelling list in her lap.

"Those are page three words," said Jessica. "It's page four that gets me. Like *heirloom.* I keep spelling it HAIR-loom."

"Those are like *fourth*-grade words," said Judy.

When their main courses came, Stink said, "Even vegetables taste good on a stick."

"Stink would eat *camel* on a stick,"

said Judy. "Hey, Jessica? Can you spell *KABOBBLEHEAD?*"

Just then, Judy dropped her mini-meat-ball kabob. It landed—*SPLAT!*—right smack-dab in the middle of her lap! On her lap was not a napkin, but . . . Jessica's spelling list! Page four. Judy swiped at the spelling list with her napkin.

Yikes-a-roni! Page four now had a big fat meatball smudge that would not budge. Judy flipped the list back to page one. Good thing they were done studying. She slid the list across the table toward Jessica's plate.

@   @   @

When they got to the hotel, Mom and Dad checked them in. They stood in line behind a guy with a pet iguana named Iggy. A kid walked past them in the lobby with a chinchilla on a leash.

"This is the coolest hotel ever!" said Judy.

"Check out the glass elevator," said Stink, pointing.

"It's like the Eiffel Tower."

"It's like *Charlie and the Great Glass Elevator*," said Stink. "Maybe we'll get to ride with Oompa-Loompas."

"Try to get a room on the seventh floor," Judy told her parents.

"That's where our room is!" said Jessica.

"Seven is good luck," said Judy. "Maybe that means you'll win the spelling bee!"

"Oh, yeah. Don't forget I need my spelling list back," said Jessica.

"Spelling list?" said Judy. "I don't have your list. I thought *you* had your list."

"I don't have my list. I thought *you* had my list."

Judy shook her head no.

"We started eating. We were done spelling. So I gave it back to you." A prickle of guilt made Judy's face grow hot. She did not mention the Meatball Smudge Incident. But that's how she knew she had given the list back. She remembered wiping the smudge, flipping the list back to page one, and passing it across the table to Jessica.

"What am I gonna do?" Jessica wailed.

"Judy? Is this true?" asked Mom.

"Did you forget Jessica's list at the restaurant?" asked Mrs. Finch.

"I didn't forget it," said Judy. "I gave the list back to her. *She* forgot it."

Fink-Face Finch squinted her beady eyes at Judy.

"You're a bad-luck charm, Judy Moody."

"Am not!"

"If you don't want me to win," Jessica sniffed, "just say so."

"Mom!" said Judy. "That is so not true. Honest!"

"No worries," said Mom. "Let's just call the restaurant and find out if someone found the list."

"But what if—I mean—" Jessica was tearing up, half-sobbing. "What if they threw it in the T-R-A-S-H?"

Mr. Finch called KaBob's Place. Mr. Finch said, "Uh-huh, uh-huh."

"Good news. We're in luck!" said Mr. Finch, after he hung up the phone. "The waitress found the list on our table. They're holding it at the cash register."

"Jessica has a big day tomorrow," said Dad. "Why don't you go up to your room and relax. Judy and I will go back and get the list. We're more than happy to help, right Judy?"

Judy half-nodded. Fink-Face Finch sure knew how to turn on the waterworks and make everybody think she had done this on purpose. It was on-top-of-spaghetti way-not-fair.

ROAR! *Where was the Growly House when you needed it?*

Just when she'd been starting to think Jessica was an UN-fink, too. She'd like to give that Jessica Finch a Shampoo Banana.

When Judy and Dad came back from KaBob's Place with the spelling list, Mom said, "Honey, take it over to Jessica. They're right across the hall in room 711."

There were exactly three things wrong with that plan.

1.) Judy still wanted to give Fink-Face
Finch a HAIRLOOM full of banana.

2.) There was still that big fat kabob blob smack in the middle of page four.

3.) Jessica A. Freakazoid would go nuts when she saw the blob.

"Mom, I might have spilled a kabob on page four. Do you think she'll notice?"

"Let me see." Stink took a look at the list. "Oh, she'll notice. This looks like it was on the *Titanic—after* it sank."

"Stink, you're not helping," said Dad.

Judy snatched the list out of Stink's hand. She stomped across the hall. She stood outside the door and rubbed her lucky penny. *Don't be mad. Don't be mad.* Maybe she'd get lucky and Jessica would not turn to page four.

Judy knocked on the door. "Room service!" she called.

Jessica opened the door. Mr. and Mrs. Finch were watching TV. PeeGee WeeGee was curled up asleep on Jessica's bed.

"Here's your list." Judy handed it over. The list was wrinkled. The list was crinkled. The list looked like it had just survived a food fight. Or a tsunami. Or a tsunami food fight.

Jessica started to flip through the pages. Some luck.

"I may have spilled

a little something on page four," Judy blurted.

"A *little* something?" Jessica wailed. "I can't read half these words. What if the winning word is under this smudge? I could lose the whole spelling bee because of this. Which means our whole class could lose. Our whole school could lose."

"I'm VERY BERRY FURRY MERRY CHERRY HONEY BUNNY FUNNY sorry."

"Why do you have to Judy-Moody-ruin everything?" Jessica said, sighing.

"I didn't do it on purpose," Judy said in a low voice.

Jessica crossed her arms. She dug her foot into the carpet.

Judy's ears burned. Her mouth felt like

sand. "Go ahead. Don't believe me," she croaked. "I'm going to emancipate from you if that'll make you happy."

"Huh?"

"Emancipate. It means to *set free.* I'm free now. Free from being your Study Buddy. And you're free, too. Free from my bad luck."

Jessica's mouth hung open. "What are you saying? I don't get it."

"Then let me spell it out. E-M-A-N-C-I-P-A-T-E." Judy stormed across the hall. "Do you want me to use it in a sentence?"

Judy Moody, Pig Sitter

The next morning, Judy peered through the peephole in the hotel door that looked out into the hall. All she could see was nothing. All she could hear was the slam of the door from last night after she got mad at Jessica.

Judy sat on the edge of the foldout bed. She, Judy Moody, was a cruddy Study

Buddy. Now Jessica would think she was a crummy pig sitter, too. She twirled and twisted her hair until it made a big fat knot. Ouch.

Knock knock!

She leaped up and ran to the door.

Jessica Finch. Plus one potbellied piggy on a leash!

Judy forgot she was still mad. "PeeGee WeeGee!" she said, throwing open the door. Judy bent down to scratch the piggy's ears. PeeGee WeeGee snuffled the carpet. PeeGee WeeGee turned in circles. PeeGee WeeGee curled his tail. "At least somebody's happy to see me."

Jessica had her hair in a special pig-tail. And she was wearing a pink skirt and a shirt that had a picture of a pig. It said I'M WITH HIM. "I know you want to *emancipate* from me and everything," said Jessica. "But I still need you to baby-sit my pig."

"I thought *you* wanted to emancipate from *me*, too," said Judy.

"I did. I do. But you made a piggy promise," said Jessica. "Besides, I can't take a *pig* to a spelling *bee.*" Jessica snorted and laughed like a hyena.

Once upon a lucky penny, Judy had wanted to be in the spelling bee herself. But now she was happy to be a pig sitter. "C'mon, PeeGee WeeGee," said Judy, taking the leash. "We are going to have way more fun than any old spelling bee, aren't we?" PeeGee WeeGee snuffled her mussy hair.

Stink came to the door. He scratched under the piggy's ears. "Remember me?"

"I call him P.G. for short," said Jessica. "Hold on." She ran back to her room. She came back carrying boatloads of pig stuff.

"Here's his water dish. Make sure he has fresh water at all times."

"Check," said Judy.

"Here's his busy ball. Pig pellets come out, in case he gets hungry. I forgot Binky, his favorite stuffed animal. But here's his favorite blankie if he wants to take a nap."

"Check," said Judy.

"He likes this pillow, too." She handed

Judy a pillowcase filled with beans. "He curls up on it. Oh, and this is special shampoo in case you want to give him a bath."

"Does he have a favorite song, like 'On Top of Spaghetti?'" Judy teased.

"Oops! I almost forgot." She ran away and came back waving a piece of notebook paper. "His favorite song is 'This Little Piggy' but these are the words he likes better. I wrote them out for you."

Judy looked at Stink and made the cuckoo sign.

Mr. and Mrs. Finch came out of their room across the hall. "Time to go, honey," said Mrs. Finch. "The spelling bee starts in one hour. Judy, do you and Stink have everything you need?"

Judy nodded. "I'm good with pigs," she said.

The Moodys stepped out into the hall. "Just do your best today," Mom said to Jessica. "You're going to be great."

"Class 3T will be proud," said Dad.

"Thanks," said Jessica. "Wish me luck."

"Break a leg," said Stink.

"I hope not!" said Jessica.

"Well, then, break a pigtail," said Judy. She cracked herself up.

Jessica leaned down to give P.G. one more hug. "Don't let P.G. eat candy bars," she called over her shoulder.

"Say hi to Mr. Todd!" Judy called back.

"Oh, and TV kind of freaks him out," Jessica added, "unless it's the movie *Babe*."

"Don't worry about P.G.," said Mom. "The kids will take good care of him."

As soon as Jessica and her parents were gone, Judy threw her hands in the air and yelled, "Let's have a piggy party!"

"Kids," said Dad. "Keep P.G. in here. Mom and I will be right outside on the balcony if you need us."

"Sure," said Judy.

PeeGee WeeGee stood in a corner, shaking.

"What's wrong with him?" Stink asked.

"I think he's scared," said Judy.

P.G. raised one eyebrow and grunted. All of a sudden, Judy smelled a terrible, no-good, very bad smell.

"Stink-*er!*" said Judy.

"It wasn't me," said Stink. "It was the pig. I read in the *P* encyclopedia that pigs can let go an awful smell when they're scared."

Judy cracked open a window. "We should call him P.U." Judy said. "Not P.G."

Judy and Stink sat on the floor across from each other and rolled the busy ball back and forth between them. After a few minutes, P.G. quieted down and stopped quivering.

"Try rolling the ball to him now, Stink."

P.G. raised his ears. He chased after the ball. The ball rolled under the bed.

P.G. dove in after it and came out the other side.

"Good boy, P.G.," said Judy. She scooped up the ball and shook it. "Little pellets are supposed to fall out for him to eat."

"Do you think he's hungry?" asked Stink.

"Pigs are always hungry," said Judy.

Stink ate some chips from a bag. P.G. went bananas, tearing around the room.

"Stink! He can't have candy. Put that away! You're making him all cuckoo."

"It's not candy. It's chips."

"Whatever. The noisy bag sound is driving him crazy."

"He wants something in your suit-case," said Stink. P.G. had Judy's polka-dot kneesock in his mouth.

"P.G.! Give that back!" said Judy. "You are all nose, you know that?"

"Look," said Stink. "He's trying to open the mini fridge!"

Judy picked up the phone and pressed a button. "Room service?" she asked. "Do you have any pig food?"

Judy listened. "Uh-huh. Uh-huh." She nodded. "Cottage cheese? Sounds good. Yogurt? Sounds healthy." She nodded some more. "Thanks!"

"I know," said Judy. "Let's give P.G. a bath while we wait for the pig food."

Judy filled the tub with a little bit of warm water. "And now, for some piggy shampoo." She made the water sudsy, like a bubble bath. "In you go," she said.

P.G. kicked. P.G. splashed. P.G. jumped. "Look! He loves it," said Judy.

"Too bad we don't have a rubber ducky. I mean rubber *piggy*," said Stink.

"Stink, squeeze some shampoo on him and I'll rub it in." Stink ran to get the shampoo bottle.

"Scrub-a-dub-dubby, P.G. loves the tubby," Judy sang. P.G. snorted and squealed.

"That's not one of the songs he likes," said Stink.

"This little piggy went to D.C. . . . ." Judy sang.

She rinsed him off. "There. Squeaky clean," she said. She tried to lift him out of the tub, but P.G. was all wet and wiggly. Soapy and squiggly.

"Help, Stink. Grab a towel. He's super slippery."

Stink came over and held out the towel. Judy picked up the piglet. That pig was extra squiggly. That pig was extra wiggly.

"Mr. Piggle Wiggle," said Judy. Before she could get P.G. into the towel, that little piggy squiggled and wiggled right out of Judy's arms.

That little piggy bolted right out of the bathroom. P.G. ran out into the front room. He ran right out the door and into the hall.

"Who left the door open?" Judy called.

Judy ran after the pig. Stink ran after Judy, still holding the towel. P.G. snorted and squealed and bumped into walls. They chased that pig down the fancy carpet past paintings of cherry blossoms. They chased that pig past a calico cat with a tiara. They chased that pig to the big red EXIT sign.

"PeeGee WeeGee! Come back here!" Judy called.

Ding! Judy heard a bell. *OH, NO! E-L-E-V-A-T-O-R! Elevator!*

"Hurry, Stink! We have to get him before he goes on the—PEEGEE WEEGEE! NOoooooo!"

P.G. was on the elevator!

Whoosh! The doors closed shut. P.G. was riding the elevator!

"Stink!" cried Judy. "Why didn't you grab him with the towel?"

"Are you kidding? Wet pigs are as slippery as greased lightning. And fast. We better go tell Mom and Dad what happened."

"I'm telling Mom and Dad," said Judy, "when pigs fly!"

"But maybe they can put out a pig alert in the hotel or something."

"Or something!" Judy looked at the numbers above the elevator door. Up, up, up it went. "C'mon, Stink. He's going up. We have to catch him before—"

Stink pointed. "Now he's coming back down! The elevator is probably going all the way to the lobby!"

"I got it!" said Judy. "The stairs!"

Judy and Stink pushed through the door to the stairwell. They ran down one-two-three flights of stairs. They ran down four-five-six flights of stairs.

When they got to the bottom, Judy bent over, breathing hard. "Why did we have to get a room on the seventh floor?" Judy asked.

"Because you said seven is a lucky number," said Stink.

"Well, it sure turned out to be UN-lucky," said Judy.

They opened the door onto a hallway and turned a corner to reach the lobby.

The lobby was empty. Pigless. All the elevator doors were closed.

No sign of pig anywhere. Not one hair. Not even a pig tail.

Pig in the City

"He's not here!" Judy cried. "What are we going to do?"

She, Judy Moody, had all the luck. *NOT*. P.G. was L-O-S-T *lost*.

"Maybe he got off on another floor," said Stink.

Ding! Just then, an elevator door opened. Judy and Stink rushed over and peered inside. A guy in a bathrobe and slippers stepped out.

"Have you seen a pig?" Judy asked the guy. "He's about this big, pinkish, with a black spot on his tail. He answers to the name PeeGee WeeGee or just P.G.?"

"Sorry. My ride was pig-free," said the guy, heading for the pool.

Ding! Another elevator landed. Only a gray-haired lady with an umbrella stepped out.

"He's got to be around here some-where," said Judy. "C'mon, Stinker. Think like a pig."

"I'm hungry," said Stink.

"Not now, Stink."

"But you told me to think like a pig.

Pigs are always hungry." Stink cupped his hand to his mouth. "Mar-co!" he called.

"Oink-o," Judy called back.

"It's *Polo*," said Stink.

"Um, Stink, I hate to tell you, but pigs can't say 'Polo.'"

"Oh. Yeah."

Judy slumped to the floor. It was no use. Her lucky penny must be deader than a toenail. O-U-T out of good luck. All it seemed to bring now was the other kind. B-A-D luck.

"C'mon, Stink. If you were a pig in a big hotel, where would you go?"

"To the piggy bank?" Stink teased.

"Get serious."

"Okay, I'd ride piggyback on one of those wheelie carts all the way down to the pool. Then I'd climb up the high dive and—"

"When pigs fly!" said Judy. Wait a second. *Fly?* She looked up. Of course! The glass elevator. "Follow me!"

Judy and Stink stood smack-dab in the center of the lobby. They looked up, up, up at the fancy glass elevator. "Is that who I think it is?" Stink asked.

It was not an iguana named Iggy. It was not a chinchilla. It was not an Oompa Loompa. It was a little piggy running in circles around the inside of the glass elevator.

"P.G.!" called Judy. *Hurry up! Hurry up!* she willed the elevator. "Why does that thing have to take so long?"

Ding! At last, the elevator landed and the door opened. P.G. was chasing his tail and kicking up his pig's feet.

"Hold the door open," Judy told Stink. She talked baby talk to P.G. "Who's a bad little piggy? You are. Yes you are. Coo, coo, coo."

"*You're* cuckoo," said Stink.

Just then, P.G. bolted out the elevator door, away from Judy, and past Stink. *Oink! Oink! Snort!* He ran squealing and grunting, slipping and sliding across the marble lobby floors. He ran over to a potted tree in the lobby and snuffled in the dirt.

"Dirt! He misses dirt!" said Stink.

Pshoo! P.G. sneezed and shook his ears. He ran circles around the fountain in the lobby.

"P.G.! No!" said Judy, but it was too late. *Ker-splash!* P.G. bounded right in.

"Towel time," said Judy, taking the towel from Stink. "Okay. I'm going to sneak up behind him and grab him." Tiptoe . . . tiptoe . . . tiptoe . . . *pounce!*

"Gotcha!" said Judy. She scooped P.G. up in the towel and snuggled him close. "P.G., what were you thinking? You already had a bath, you nutty pig."

Judy, Stink, and P.G. got back on the elevator. Stink pressed the button for seven. "Going up!" he called.

"You had us worried there, P.G.," said Judy. "Yes you did." She held P.G. in the air and rubbed noses with him. "Gimme a kiss!" she cooed.

When they got back, Dad poked his head into the room. "Where were you two?"

"Um, we just took P.G. for a ride on the elevator," said Judy. "No biggie."

"Next time, *ask* before you leave this room," said Mom. "Both of you."

"And who ordered all this cottage cheese?" asked Dad.

"We did. It's for P.G.," said Judy. *Snarf!* P.G. was already helping himself.

"All right. I have to make a call and check in with Grandma Lou. We'll be in here if you need us," said Mom.

When P.G. was done snarfing his food, he hopped up on the bed and curled up on his special pillow. Judy wrapped him in his favorite blankie, where he snuggled with Blue Monkey. *"This little piggy rode an elevator,"* she sang softly.

Stink flipped on the TV. P.G. shook his head till his ears flapped, and backed away.

"Stink! TV freaks him out, and I just got him to settle down."

"Sorry," said Stink. He hit the mute

button, flipping through channels.

"Remember, P.G.," Judy whispered. "No squealing on us when Jessica gets back, okay? The elevator ride? That's our little secret. Shake on it?" Judy picked up his right hoof and shook.

"Hey, look what's on!" Stink cried. "The sequel to his favorite movie. *Babe: Pig in the City!*"

"You are one lucky-ducky pig," Judy told P.G. She cuddled up with him to watch the movie. Stink turned up the sound.

"And there's Farmer Hoggett," said Judy. "He got hurt. And now Babe has to try to save the farm." They all three watched the movie. Judy and Stink laughed. "See? Babe got to stay in a hotel, too. Just like you."

"*Mmmph!*" P.G. snorted.

"Look. He's getting sleepy," said Stink.

"He's had a big day," said Judy. "He's P.G.: Pig in the City."

E-M-A-N-C-I-P-A-T-E

Zzzzz. At last, PeeGee WeeGee started to snooze. *Snurf!*

"Phew. We lucked out. He fell asleep. Doesn't he look all cute when he's sleeping?" Judy whispered.

"His eyes are moving. I think he's dreaming," said Stink.

"Visions of cottage cheese are dancing in his head," said Judy.

"Visions of *elevators*," said Stink.

"Shh!" Judy warned. Jessica Finch

could be right outside that door. It was almost four. Jessica might be coming back any minute. "No squealing about the ride on the You-Know-What!" said Judy, putting her finger to her lips.

Knock knock!

Judy jumped up and opened the door. Sure enough, it was Jessica Finch. And she had a bee painted on her face. A *spelling* bee.

"How did the spelling bee—" Judy started to ask, but Jessica ran over to P.G.

"Don't wake him up. I just got him—"

Too late. Jessica had already scooped P.G. up in her arms and was giving him hugs and kisses. "P.G.!" she said. "I missed you, you little pig face."

"*PeeGee WeeGee!*" squealed P.G. He curled his tail.

"Aw, you missed me, too, didn't you, little guy?" Jessica cooed.

Mr. and Mrs. Finch came up behind Jessica. They peered inside. The Moody's hotel room was a mess. The bed was a tornado. Socks and shoes littered the floor. Trays with empty bowls of cottage cheese were here, there, and everywhere.

"What happened here?" Mr. Finch asked.

"This place is a pigsty!" said Jessica, cackling.

"Duh!" said Judy. "He's *your* pig. You know how he is."

"I'm afraid we do," said Mrs. Finch.

Mom and Dad came out of the other room when they heard the commotion.

"The kids really had a fun time with P.G.," said Dad.

"We gave P.G. a bath," said Stink.

"And I taught him to give kisses," said Judy.

"And P.G. didn't escape or ride the elevator or anything," said Stink.

Judy gave Stink the stink-eye. "Squealer!" she muttered under her breath. She quick-changed the subject. "Hurry up, Jessica. Tell us what happened at the spelling bee."

"It was fine."

"Fine?" Judy screeched. "That's it?" Judy wagged her finger at Jessica. "Wait a second. I get it. It's okay if you didn't win, you know."

"Yeah, but, okay, um . . . I did win."

"You WON?" said Judy. "As in *won*? As in beat everybody? Even Sanjay Sharma? As in Class 3T and Virginia Dare School takes home the trophy for The Great Third-Grade Spelling Bee?"

Jessica nodded.

"See, told you you'd win! Even though I kabobbed your spelling list."

"Can you believe it? Our girl won," said Mr. Finch.

"We're so proud of her," said Mrs. Finch.

"Congratulations, Jessica!" said Mom.

"Way to go!" said Dad.

"Where's the trophy?" Stink asked.

"Then I don't get it," said Judy. "Why are you acting weird?"

"I'm not acting weird," said Jessica.

"Yes you are. You should be going crazy and running laps around the room and screaming 'I won, I won' and jumping up and down on furniture and stuff."

"Go ahead, honey. Tell us all about it," said Mom.

"Well, first I spelled *cartoon* and *nightmare.*"

"Easy-peasy," said Judy. "For you, I mean."

"Then it got harder. I got flip-flops in my stomach when they said *unbelievable* because I couldn't remember if it was *I* before *E* or *E* before *I.*"

"Or *E-I-E-I-O,*" said Stink. Everybody laughed.

"Then it got down to just me and Sanjay. I thought for sure he was going to win. I was so nervous my teeth were chattering like it was the middle of winter."

"What word did you win with?" Judy asked.

"Was it *titanic?*" Stink asked.

"Was it *gargantuan?*" Judy asked. "I bet it was *gargantuan.*"

"Was it *president?*" Stink asked. "No wait, was it *jawbreaker?* It was *jawbreaker,* wasn't it?"

Jessica shrugged.

Mr. Finch said, "Her mother and I were worried because it wasn't on any of the lists."

"We still don't know how she knew it," said Mrs. Finch.

Jessica's pigtail bounced as she looked from her mom to her dad

"Go ahead. Tell them your word, sweetheart," said Mrs. Finch.

Jessica dug her shoe into the carpet. She whispered something Judy couldn't quite hear.

Judy leaped up. "What? Did you say—"

"*Emancipate,*" said Jessica, a little

louder. "Okay? Are you happy? The word was *EMANCIPATE!*"

"*Emancipate!*" Judy cried. She could not help cracking up.

"Hey!" Stink ran over and grabbed Abe Lincoln. "That's like the word on my second-favorite-president statue. I just got it yesterday."

"Same-same!" said Judy. "Good thing Jessica didn't spell *eman-ci-potato*."

"What a coincidence," said Dad.

"It's an UNBELIEVABLE co-inky-dink. Rare!" said Judy.

"You're on a lucky strike, Jessica," said Stink. "Like Judy."

"*Streak*," said Judy. "Lucky *streak*."

"Did you see it on my statue and that's how you knew?" said Stink. "So I helped you win?"

"Actually," Jessica admitted. "It was Judy."

"It was me who said you, Jessica Finch, can spell even fifth-grade words. In fact, I bet you could spell the whole entire dictionary!"

"Thanks," said Jessica. "Sorry I was such an aardvark."

"Aardwolf," said Judy.

"Whatever. I was just so nervous and worried about the spelling bee—"

"It's okay. Sorry I was such a meatball. I kabobbed your spelling list. Right over the important words, too."

"*Meatball* was one of the spelling-bee words!" said Jessica.

"No way!" said Judy.

"Hey, I have an idea," said Dad. "Let's emancipate ourselves from this hotel and go get some ice cream at Pitango to celebrate. What do you say?"

"Then can we go to the Old Post Office?" asked Judy. "They have a bell tower and you can climb up it and see way far away."

"I read that the clock tower has some of the best views of the city," said Mom.

"Great idea!" said Mr. Finch. Mrs. Finch nodded.

"P.G. likes ice cream," said Jessica.

"I scream, you scream, we all scream for ice cream," sang Stink, leading the way.

☙   ☙   ☙

The next morning, it was time to head home. Outside on the sidewalk in front of the hotel, the Moodys said good-bye to the Finches for what seemed like an hour. Bor-ing.

At last, the Finches' car pulled away. Judy ran down the sidewalk all the way to the curb, waving and blowing kisses to P.G.

When the car was out of sight, Judy reached into her pocket to make a new wish on her lucky penny.

What! No penny?

She reached down deeper. Fooey Louie. She reached into every corner, but all she got was lint. She checked all her other pockets. Twice.

She spun around, looking here, there, and everywhere. She checked the cracks in the sidewalk. She even searched her shoe.

No luck. The lucky penny was nowhere.
She checked her pocket one last time.
That's when she found it.
   A hole!

Her lucky penny was GFG. Gone For Good. Emancipated. Set free. Was losing a lucky penny bad luck? What if she never had good luck again?

All of a sudden, a flashing light at the intersection caught her eye. Two cop cars pulled up, stopping traffic.

Judy squinted down the street, into the bright light. Just then, she thought she saw—Could it be? Were her eyes playing tricks on her? *No!*

"Guys! Guys!" she yelled down the sidewalk, trying to get her family's attention. Judy rushed back to the car, banging on the window to get Mom and Stink's attention. Dad had his head in the trunk, wrestling with the luggage.

She jumped up and down, pointing and stabbing the air. "It's him! For real! Did you see? Did you?"

"Who him?" asked Stink. He scrambled out of the car, climbed up on a bench and peered down the street. "All I see are a bunch of black cars."

"*Secret agent* black cars," said Judy. "It was him! The present. I mean president. He just jogged down that cross street. No lie!"

"Looks like the president's motorcade," said Dad.

"He must be out exercising," said Mom.

"I can't believe I missed it!" Stink told

Judy. "You saw a for-real president. No fair. You have all the luck."

"But I don't—" Judy started to say, thinking about losing her lucky penny.

Hey, wait just a lucky-ducky minute! She did have good luck without her lucky penny. Cool-o-roonie!

❀   ❀   ❀

As they pulled away, Judy gazed out the back window of the car until the Washington Monument was nothing but a teeny tiny dot. A speck on the horizon.

She waved good-bye to the District of Cool.

She, Judy Moody, was a VERY BERRY FURRY MERRY FUNNY BUNNY LUCKY DUCKY. She got to go on a runaway pig adventure, help win the Great Third-Grade Spelling Bee, and even become real friends with Jessica Finch.

And she got a present. The present of seeing the president!

Megan McDonald is the author of the popular Judy Moody and Stink series, as well as the Judy Moody and Friends series for new readers. She has written many other books for children, including the Ant and Honey Bee stories, the Sisters Club series, and several picture books. Before she began writing full-time, Megan McDonald worked as a librarian, a bookseller, and a living-history actress. She lives in Northern California with her husband, Richard Haynes, who is also a writer.

Peter H. Reynolds is the illustrator of the popular Judy Moody and Stink series in addition to many other books, including several for which he is also author. They include his Creatrilogy of picture books: *The Dot, Ish,* and *Sky Color.* His book *The Dot* has even inspired International Dot Day, which is celebrated around the world every September. Besides writing and illustrating, Peter H. Reynolds is a bookstore owner, animator, and educator. He lives in Massachusetts with his family.

Dear Megan McDonald, would you rather:

Eat the world's largest jawbreaker or a Screamin' Mimi's ice-cream cone?

I think I'm already the proud owner of the World's Largest Jawbreaker, so I'd have to choose a Screamin' Mimi's ice-cream cone. Besides, the real Screamin' Mimi's is in my hometown!

Have a bowl of Mood Flakes or a plate of silver-dollar pancakes for breakfast?

I've got plenty of moods already, so I'm with Stink—silver-dollar pancakes are the best!

Wear a Sybil Ludington costume or a Nancy Drew outfit?

Sybil Ludington, the Revolutionary War hero who rode twice as far as Paul Revere, was a real historical figure. I've always admired her courage and pluck. I'd choose to dress like her any day!

Solve a mystery or solve a math word problem?

My favorite books to read are mysteries, so it's no mystery which I'd choose. I love trying to solve the mystery before the book is over.

Read a book or write a book?

Help! I LOVE BOTH!

Get a for-real glimpse of the Loch Ness monster or of Bigfoot?

Bigfoot! He drives an ice-cream truck, right?

Dear Peter H. Reynolds, would you rather:

Eat a peanut-butter cup or chocolate-covered raisins?

I'd take the chocolate-covered raisins because my twin brother, Paul, loves peanut-butter cups—so I am sure he'd share with me!

Drink a cup of tea or a mug of coffee?

Having grown up in a very British home, I would rather drink tea. I also love painting with tea!

Have a Boston Tub Party or go on a Midnight Zombie Walk?

I grew up and live in the Boston area, so hands down, I'd rather have a Boston Tub Party. In fact, from my studio at FableVision, I have a view of the Boston Tea Party ship.

Take a trip to Argentina or a trip to Antarctica?

I've already been to Argentina a bunch of times. My dad was born there in a town called Tandil. I have been dreaming about visiting Antarctica for a long time. I even have a travel brochure pinned to my Dream Board in my studio, aka the Sanctuary.

Draw a picture of Judy Moody or a picture of Stink?

What a tough choice! It's almost a tie, but I have to say, I am always amazed at how few lines it takes to create Stink. His hair looks like a lawn. I'm going to have to say Stink. (Don't tell Judy!)

Get a for-real glimpse of the Loch Ness monster or of Bigfoot?

Bigfoot scares me. The Loch Ness monster would dip back below the water and I'd be safe on shore—so I choose Nessie.

Judy Moody Slang Dictionary

From *double rare* to *star-spangled bananas,* here's a look at some of Judy Moody's favorite expressions. With this Judy Moody slang dictionary, you'll never be at a loss for words—and that's definitely double cool!

rare!: cool!

double rare!: way cool!

double cool!: twice as cool!

ROAR!: what to say when you're angry or frustrated

pizza table: the little plastic piece that keeps a pizza from touching the top of the pizza box

bothers: little brothers who bother you all the time!

smad: sad and mad, at the same time!

same-same: what you say when you and your friend do something that's the same

phoney baloney: fake

not-boring: interesting

boing!: aha!

star-spangled bananas!: what you say when you're surprised or amazed

L.B.S.: Long Boring Story

Ouch Face: the face you make when someone's pulling your hair

ABC gum: Already Been Chewed gum

nark: bad mood

T. P. Club: the Toad Pee Club

oogley: gross

caterpillar eyebrow: the way your eyebrows look when you're in a mood (not a good mood, a bad mood!)

or something: what you say when someone presents you with a list of choices that end with "or something" and you don't agree with any of the choices

V.I.Q.: Very Important Question

Antarctica: the desk at the back of Mr. Todd's classroom where you have to sit if you're causing trouble

goopy: cheesy

BE SURE TO CHECK OUT STINK'S ADVENTURES!

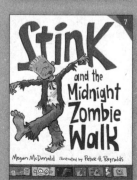

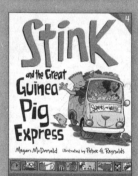

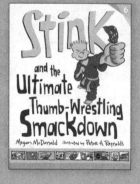

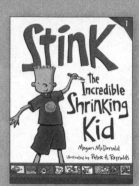

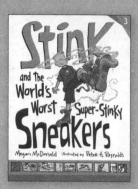

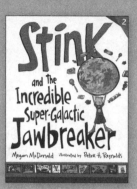

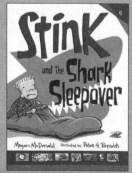

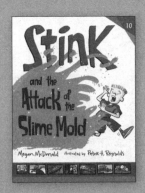

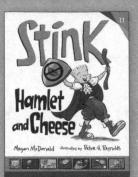

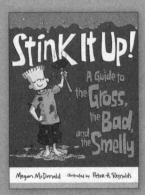

JUMP-START YOUR STINK COLLECTION WITH BOXED SETS —
EACH OFFERING A TRIO OF PAPERBACK TITLES:

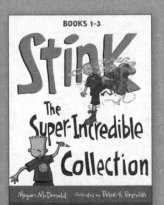

Judy Moody and Stink are starring together!

In full color!

New to the Moody universe?

Try a boxed set of the first three full-color books starring Judy Moody and Stink in paperback!

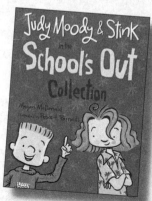